The Tlytiettlym Tree

By Alena Netia Horowitz

Illustrations by Alena Netia Horowitz
and Mary De La Fuente

First American Edition

Cover designed by Alena Netia Horowitz and Mary De La Fuente
Manufactured in the Singapore

10 9 8 7 6 5 4 3 2 1

The text of this book is set in 14 point Times New Roman.
The illustrations are rendered in colored pencils.

Library of Congress Cataloging-in-Publication Data
Horowitz, Alena Netia;
The Tlytiettlym Tree/Alena Netia Horowitz;
Illustrated by Alena Netia Horowitz and Mary De La Fuente.
1st American ed.   p.   cm.
Summary: A group of fourth graders learn to work together
with patience and love in their quest to find a magical tree
growing fruits that produce miraculous healings and possibly world peace.
ISBN: 0-923550-42-9
[1. Social skills   Fiction; 2. Spiritual healing   Fiction]

Card Number and
Additional cataloging data pending.

Additional copies of this book are available for bulk purchases.
For more information, please contact:
Tetrahedron, LLC • Suite 147, 206 North 4th Avenue • Sandpoint, Idaho 83864
1-888-508-4787, Fax: 208-265-2775, E-mail: tetra@tetrahedron.org,
URL web site: http://www.tetrahedron.org

DEDICATED TO THOSE WHO HELP
CHILDREN AND FAMILIES
CHALLENGED BY AUTISM.

The Tlytiettlym Tree

Contents

Foreword

The *Tlytiettlym Tree* (pronounced Tly-tit-a-lum) was written by a nine-year-old fourth grader—Alena Netia Horowitz—who determined to write a book to help raise money to fly her Waldorf School class cross-country. She dreamed of performing "The Kalevala, a Finnish Epic," along with her classmates, for the benefit of autistic and special needs children living in other states. With the publication of this book, her dream may, indeed, come true.

This story was actually conceived by Alena during a trip to Washington, D.C. in which she had the opportunity to care for several autistic children during a national U.S. Autism Ambassador's conference. The meeting was conducted in April, 2002, in connection with a U.S. Government Reform Committee hearing into autistic spectrum disorder, and the apparent link between this rapidly growing epidemic, and vaccinations containing mercury.

Two weeks earlier, I—Alena's dad—had taken her to see Paul McCartney in concert at the MGM Grand in Las Vegas, Nevada. Nearly everyone might say that a child who gets to see Paul McCartney in concert once is *very* fortunate. Alena, however, was more than that. On our one free evening during the autism conference, I took Alena again to McCartney's "Driving Rain" concert, this time in Philadelphia. We drove three hours, each way, between cities that night, and it was there that the seed was planted for the creation of *The Tlytiettlym Tree*.

Concert goers typically appreciate the highly spirited comraderee that commonly develops during a rock concert. In Philadelphia there were two couples seated directly behind us whom we befriended. They had children too that unfortunately were unable to attend. They missed their little angels terribly, so they adopted Alena as a niece for those few hours.

What struck these couples, most amazingly, about Alena was that she foretold virtually every song McCartney sang in a similar sequence to his performance in Las Vegas. They were heart-struck. Here was a nine-year-old child who not only knew the names of Beatles' songs more than thirty years old, but could accurately predict the next song he was about to sing.

Seconds before McCartney's very last song of the night, Alena told our new friends, "This is *the end*. This is the last song he's going to sing."

In that highly spirited moment, Alena did not realize that she had actually *named* McCartney's final song—"The End"—a cut from Abbey Road. The song finishes with McCartney singing his famous lyrics: "And in the end, the love you take is equal to the love you make."

A dedicated McCartney and Beatles fan, her closest buddy in the group turned to Alena and said, "Sweetheart, you remember the last words that Paul is going to sing in this song. They will be the most important words, and most valuable lesson, you will ever learn in your entire life."

We left the concert completely uplifted. When we got to the car, Alena asked me. "Daddy, what did that nice man mean when he said that about Paul McCartney's last words?"

"He meant exactly what the words say," I replied. "'The love you take is equal to the love you make' means the amount of love you experience in your life depends on the amount of people you touch with your love and loving deeds." Alena apparently got the message.

The following afternoon, as I testified on behalf of children and families affected by autism during Dan Burton's congressional investigative hearing on Capitol Hill, rather than following the proceedings, Alena was engaged in making a contribution of her own, likewise intended to help end devastating vaccine-initiated autism. She sat at a desk, with paper and pencil in hand, in the very back of the hearings chamber, feverishly writing.

When the hearing closed, I walked over to Alena, still energetically writing, "What are you doing, love?"

"I'm writing a book, dad," she replied.

"Is that right? What's it about?" I asked.

"It's about two groups of children—good ones and nasty ones. They form two clubs. The nice children find a treasure map that leads them to a magical tree that has all the fruits of the entire world on it. But, to gather the fruit, the children, who have been fighting, need to get along, love each other, and cooperate.

"I want to write and sell the book to raise money to fly my class to the autistic children's school to present our play."

"That's wonderful sweetheart," I replied. "Do you have a name for your book?"

"I want to call it *The Tlytiettlym Tree.*"

Alena's book title—**The Tlytiettlym Tree**—derives from the first letters of each word of Paul McCartney's prescription for gaining more love from life. "**T**he **l**ove **y**ou **t**ake **i**s **e**qual **t**o **t**he **l**ove **y**ou **m**ake."

Obviously, as Alena's dad, I am extremely proud of her for offering this work for the benefit of children everywhere and humanity in general. As a loving parent, I am certain that you, too, will feel proud to share this story with your children, family, and friends.

By so doing, we can all contribute, as Alena has here, in spreading the wisdom of *The Tlytiettlym Tree.*

Leonard G. Horowitz, D.M.D., M.A.,M.P.H.
Author of *Healing Celebrations: Miraculous Recoveries Through Ancient Scripture, Natural Medicine and Modern Science* and *Healing Codes for the Biological Apocalypse*

The Tlytiettlym Tree

Chapter One:
Ms. Elizabeth's Class

There once was an old Victorian school house in a quaint New England town. Its peaked roof rose high above the maple trees poised between the wild blue Atlantic Ocean and the Berkshire Mountains.

It was the beginning of a new school year for the children in the fourth grade class in this private school.

Among the children, there were four girls and four boys. They were your usual friendly sort. They got along well with others, and as you might expect, they quickly learned to enjoy each other's company in this new class. In fact, by the third day of school, several of them had determined to be best friends.

Amber quickly became the leader of this pack. She was very kind to everyone, and never wanted to leave others out of activities. Her shiny brown hair was very long. She always wore it in braids. Party times were the only exception. Then she clipped her hair on both sides and let the rest hang down her back.

Kimberly was the most fun to play with. She was more mature. Her friends called her "Kimmie." She had sparkling blue eyes, and always wore colorful dresses, never pants!

Kimmie held a crush on a sixth grader Chester, or "Chazz," but he didn't have much interest in her.

Mary was the thinnest of the girls. She was part African American, and part American Indian, with short silky black hair. She was a "tomboy" who didn't care if she got dirty—the exact opposite of Kimberly. She was also a picky eater who hated things like spinach. Whenever she was offered greens, she always said, "Yuck, gross!"

Lori, the last of the four girlfriends, was a dare-devil, willing to meet virtually any challenge. She had hazel-colored eyes that everyone loved, except her. She said she wanted to dye her hair *purple*, but Amber, Kimberly and Mary always knew that she was joking.

"How about green and purple?" Amber challenged. "Then you can look like the mutant tennis balls my dad bought me."

"No way!" Mary protested, "You've got to be crazy. Buy a purple and green wig if you want to look like a de-ranged celebrity."

Among the four boys in this group of eight close friends, Adam was the "cutest." In fact, he was one of the best looking kids in the whole school. Most of the girls adored him, except Lori and Kimberly. Lori wanted him to have purple hair too. "Just kidding," she said.

Adam liked to flirt, especially with Lori and Kimberly since they liked him the least. He liked making stuff, and was especially creative, imaginative, and artistic. His drawings and paintings were all "awesome."

Cory was Adam's brown haired buddy. They lived just a few blocks away from each other, and always played together after school. Cory was not very good at sports, and Adam occasionally got frustrated and impatient with him.

Cory's special gift was his "smarts." This is what Lori appreciated most about him. She had her eye on him. When she saw Cory even talking to another girl, she got jealous. Amber, Kimberly, and Mary thought she was quite silly in that way.

John, the tallest of the four boys was "*so* cool." Everyone thought and said that. He made a great and challenging playmate, especially on the basketball court. John's big brown eyes twinkled like stars, especially after making a basket. His broad white smile seemed to lift everyone's spirits, especially their teacher's, Ms. Elizabeth.

Nick was the most athletic of the eight friends. He was taking gynmastics classes and wanted to be an acrobat. Nick had brown eyes and curly blond hair. All the girls wished they had naturally curly hair like his.

Now let me introduce the "troublemakers"— Courtney, Casey and Anthony.

They seemed unwilling, or incapable, of getting along, especially with these eight very friendly schoolmates. They dominated the class, the teacher's time, and her patience. They frequently talked back to Ms. Elizabeth, or simply gave her a hard time.

Courtney was definitely the leader of this "mean team." She liked to play tricks on others. On the first day of school, for instance, the three menaces conspired, and Courtney put a *woopy-cushion* on Ms. Elizabeth's chair. You probably know what happened. When she sat down, it sounded like she "passed gas." All the children laughed, but those three laughed the hardest.

Courtney had long dirty-blond hair that rarely looked brushed. It hung down below her waist. She often tried to make others laugh even if it was at her own expense. Like the time she told everyone that her hair fell into the toilet bowl. The outburst disturbed Ms. Elizabeth. In short, Courtney was the class clown and mischief maker.

Casey was Courtney's sidekick. She had greenish-brown eyes and wanted to be a model when she was older.

Casey *secretly* had a "crush" on John in third grade. She still sort of did. She didn't dare tell Courtney about it, though. She might then be kicked out of their "mean club," she thought.

Anthony had short curly red hair and freckles. Anthony's gifting was sports—tennis, basketball, swimming, baseball, and soccer. Everyone in the class was awed by Anthony's physical talents.

Anthony also had writing skills. He unfortunately wrote a lot of stuff that hurt people's feelings.

These two groups of children quickly became the dominant forces for good and evil within Ms. Elizabeth's fourth grade classroom. The other six children in the class didn't really fit into either of these two groups. They were just plain, shy or weird individuals who could not seem to make any friends. A good example was Billy Owens. To get students to vote for him for class president, he offered to bribe them with frogs he kept in jars!

Chapter Two:
The Fight

One day in September, Amber invited her seven close friends to come home with her after school. The special invitations were decorated with sparkles, fake jewels and glitter. Amber wrote in fancy cursive writing,

"Please come to a party at my house after school." Each card was signed, "Love, Amber."

Amber's mother "cleared" the party invitations with each of the children's parents. The only one who could not attend was John. He had a basketball game.

At the party, the children had a great time playing tag, but after awhile, some of them got very tired. So they had to think of another game to play that was not so tiring.

Adam wanted to play soccer, but Cory didn't want to play. The reason for this is because when Cory was six years old, his soccer team failed to win a single game. His insensitive coach declared that he, and the others, played like "sissies." He never forgot it, and never wanted to play soccer again. When Cory told his parents what the coach said, they immediately took him out of the league. Now he simply tells his friends, if they ask him why he doesn't want to play soccer, "I just had a bad experience when I was younger."

"Can we please?" pleaded Adam.

"But, we don't have a soccer-ball," replied Amber.

"Seriously?" interrupted Lori.

"Yup," answered Amber.

"Well then, let's play with that pink balloon," suggested Adam, pointing across the yard.

"But, it will *pop*," objected Cory.

"And besides, we stopped playing tag because we were tired remember?" reminded Mary.

With that, they all decided to think of a new game to play outside, that was fun and not so tiring.

Kimberly wanted to play her favorite game—"dress-up," including using "make-up." The second the boys heard this, they burst out laughing. Nick belittled her, "Oh my gosh! How can you want to play that?"

Kimberly explained, "You wanted a quiet game didn't you?"

"You call that a quiet game? It's more like *b o r i n g*!" Nick stuck his finger in his mouth and stuck out his tongue. Then the three boys whispered something nasty about Kimberly, chuckled rudely, and walked away. "Let's go guys," Nick directed. The trio ran off to kick the pink balloon.

All of this hurt Kimberly's feelings. She began to feel resentment against the three for making fun of her. She felt all shivery inside, but she didn't want to show her hurt feelings, so she ran away to the back-yard. There she plunked herself down on the grass under a tall shady tree and hid there for a time. Soon she felt even more shivery, so cold, in fact, and so alone, that she couldn't help but start sniffling. Her cries were just loud enough that her girlfriends could hear her in the front yard.

Amber came running. She sat down by Kimberly's side and asked, "What's the matter Kimmie?"

"Well," replied Kimberly crouched over with her head on her knees, "did you hear what they said about me?"

"Yeah," Amber answered with a heavy sigh. "I'm sorry."

"It wasn't you." Kimberly said as several big tears ran down the side of her cheek. Another droplet dripped off the tip of her nose. "*You* don't need to apologize."

Meanwhile, Nick, who was the last to kick the pink balloon before it broke, now wanted to play "hide-n-go-seek." But, everyone else scolded him, "No that game is *boring* too. Let's play something other than that."

Nick, however, didn't like to be insulted. He stormed off into the bushes at the left side of Amber's driveway determined to never be found.

Amber's mother, Alisa, inside cooking grilled cheese sandwiches for the group, saw Nick running away, but she only thought they were playing "tag" or "hide-n-go-seek."

When Nick didn't come back in a few minutes the children tried to find him. They searched the yard high and low, without luck. Lori cried out, "It's no use," and most of them stopped searching.

Now the party seemed more like a drag. Cory wanted to play "red rover." Mary didn't. They argued about this for awhile before calling each other names.

"Where could he be?" whined Amber weary of her fruitless search for Nick. "And will you two stop fighting? Two people's feelings have been hurt already, isn't that enough?"

Pulling herself together, Kimberly came to see what the commotion was all about. The two boys, Cory and Adam, saw that Kimberly's face was red. It was obvious that she had been crying.

"Oh, poor Kimmie," the boys teased. Then she ran into the house in tears once again.

Amber's mom heard the crying and headed for the

bathroom in which Kimberly sought refuge. "What is this? What's going on, Kimmie?" she asked.

Kimberly explained what had happened. Alisa walked her to Amber's bedroom, wrapped her in a warm blanket, and said, "You stay here. This party is over, unless some apologies are made."

Then Amber's mom walked outside and scolded, "You kids should think about what you have done to each other. Life's not about making enemies."

After hearing this, the children felt sad. As they thought about what Alisa had said, suddenly Cory recalled that Nick was still missing. "Hey! We forgot about Nick. Everyone, let's go find him. He might be in trouble."

With that Amber's mom became very concerned and joined the search.

When their search failed to find Nick, Amber's mom called Nick's parents. They quickly drove to Amber's house and joined the search.

When Nick, who was still hiding in the bushes, heard his father calling, "Nick, where are you?" he finally revealed himself.

"I'm over here dad," he shyly admitted.

After Nick and his parents talked about how he hurt Kimmie and how his feelings were hurt, Nick bravely walked back to the front lawn to greet the others. Everyone apologized to him, the boys apologized to Kimberly, and Mary and Cory apologized to each other.

"Everyone is forgiven," they all said.

Chapter Three:
The Birthday Party

It was almost Nick's tenth birthday, and the whole class was invited to come to his party.

His invitations where decorated with glitter, sparkles, and other fun stuff like ribbons and bows. They read on the inside, "Please come to Nick's 10th birthday party at our house on Friday, May 20th, from 3-8pm. Bring a change of clothes. You might need them. At night, we will be watching a movie and having popcorn if that's okay with all of the parents. Please respond."

Nick, and his parents, got a lot of return phone calls. Amber called and said, "Hi Nick. This is Amber. Kimmie and I are coming to your party." The others responded likewise.

Soon, the guests arrived and the party began.

The first thing the merrymakers did was hunt for treasure that Nick's mom had hidden in different parts of their yard. The hints were written with magic markers on large pieces of cardboard. These she hid in different places, like behind the barn, under the trampoline, next to the garden and orchard gates, under the picnic table, and in the barrel of chicken feed next to the hen house.

The children were divided into three teams, and the team members had to work together to understand the meanings of the written hints. For instance, the hen house hint read, "To find what you want, ask the chickens what they enjoy doing most."

There was a green team, a blue team, and a yellow one too. The treasure hunt began with Nick's mom giving the teams their first directions. Soon the teams ran off in three different directions to find their first clues.

The green team was instructed to go to the picnic table and look under it. The blue team's first clue was in the garden, in a large flower pot. The yellow team's hint was under the trampoline.

After ten minutes, or so, the green team won. They had faster runners on their side. Still, Nick's mom divided the prizes out equally. She didn't want anyone to feel hurt or left out. So, each child got two Starburst candies, a Tootsie Roll, and a lolly pop or some mints.

Then the children got more treats by batting a piñata. It split open wide when John hit it hard. Gum, red and black licorice, stickers, balloons, and a bunch of small toys seemed to rain from the sky, falling all around all over the ground inside the circle the children made. Everyone quickly grabbed for the prizes.

Next, the party goers had a water balloon fight. Nick's mother began the rumble by shouting, "Ready? One, two, three, GO!" All at once, everyone's balloons flew all across the yard. One even hit Nick's little sister, Merisa. It landed with a splot. She giggled and, to get even, grabbed a big red balloon that failed to burst on its first throw. She flung it at Mary, who hit her, and the

thing went splot all over her. She was drenched from head to toe.

Now it was Mary's turn. She saw a purple balloon on the ground below the porch where she stood. She jumped off the deck, picked it up, and hurled it at Merisa. It struck her right on her chest, and now she was soaked.

After that, all the "balloon bandits" changed into their dry clothes, and ate lunch. Nick's mom made pizza, and a veggie tray with dip. The birthday cake was an angel food cake decorated like a race track with racing cars.

Finally, it was time for Nick to open his presents. His parents gave him a tent, which really surprised and delighted him. His sister gave him a necklace she had made, a big hug, and a kiss. Amber gave him a kitten because her cat had a litter of kittens, and she couldn't keep all of them. Adam gave him a "spy ear" made from a rolled up piece of cardboard, so he could listen to other people's conversations. John gave him Legos. Kimberly gave him a bird book. Anthony gave him a rat. Courtney gave him a magic trick book. Casey gave him some Star Wars cards, and everyone else gave him an assortment of board games and art supplies.

After the party, Courtney, Anthony, and Casey had to have the last nasty word. They needled the eight best friends saying, "We have the coolest fort, and we bet you could never make one as good as ours."

Casey exaggerated, "Yeah! Not in one zillion years!"

So, the eight friends thought about it, at which point Amber whispered to the others, "Come over here." She waved the group over to the large stump next to the orchard where she sat down for a pow-wow. "Why don't we make a hide out and show those three a thing or two about who makes the best club house?"

"Yeah! Right on!!" Adam replied.

And that's precisely what they set out to do.

Chapter Four:
The Club House

About two and a half weeks later, while walking home from school, the group finally decided where they would build their fort. From school, most of the children had to follow a footpath through the woods to get back home. Much of this wooded land was owned by Nick's dad. Amber, Kimberly, Mary, Lori, Adam, Cory, John, and Nick were walking across this property when John suddenly stopped beside a big oak tree. Looking up, he burst, "Hey! Why don't we build the club house right here."

"But John, Courtney and crew have to walk past here every morning too, to get to school!" Lori objected.

"So what?" defended John.

"So, they might wreck it or laugh," argued Lori.

"Yeah, Lori's right," agreed Adam.

"I have an idea," John retorted. "If we build it on the ground, they'll get to it, but if we build it high up in this tree they'll never notice it."

"Great idea!" declared Mary. "Nick, see if your dad will allow us to use this tree. Then tomorrow, it's Friday. We can all meet right here after school. We have the whole weekend to work on the place."

Everyone agreed to the plan.

As the children started to run off toward their homes, Amber shouted, "Remember everyone, leave all the tools, wood, nails, and your sleeping bags at your

front door and I'll ask my mom to pick it all up with our truck while we're at school."

That night, Nick not only asked for his father's permission to build their fort in the old oak tree, but also if he would help the children build it. He agreed with one stipulation—that there would be no "funny business" going on in the fort.Nick promised, "Sure dad, we won't do anything weird."

The next day, the eight friends could not wait to get out of school. Unlike their usual classroom behavior, they all seemed to Ms. Elizabeth to be suffering from "attention deficit." Even the class's best students appeared antsy.

At three o'clock sharp, the usual quitting time, Mary blurted, "Oh, Ms. Elizabeth, it's three o'clock. Can we please go now?"

Determined to diagnose the source of her group's distraction, Ms. Elizabeth replied, "On the contrary, you're not leaving until someone explains to me why you've all been acting so oddly."

"Well," answered Lori, "we're making a tree house and I guess we got a little over excited."

"Yeah! We're really sorry." declared Cory, not wanting to wait a minute more. He was under the impression that a quick apology might free them from captivity.

Amber rolled her eyes at him.

"What did I do?" Cory defended.

Following a few more minutes of discussion, Ms. Elizabeth finally let them leave. They all scrambled out the door and left the school even faster. They scurried to the construction site to get started.

Amber's mother arrived with the eight sleeping bags, the tents, and most of the supplies in hand.

Amber borrowed nails, two hammers, and a handsaw from her dad's woodshop. Kimberly brought paint and paintbrushes from her father's shed. Mary found yards of rope and many leftover pieces of wood and shingles from when her family had their roof redone. Lori brought a tape measure, some pencils, a clipboard, paper, a ruler, and decorations that she liked from her mother's sewing room. Adam brought some very, very old tools that his mom or dad could no longer use for anything. He thought, *Maybe my friends can use them. If not we can hang them up on the walls of the fort.* John delivered a pulley, some metal braces and barn spikes. Cory brought rations in a cooler—two bottles of root beer, hot dogs and buns, mustard, marshmallows, cheese puffs, peaches and apples, and a bag of celery and carrots to munch on.

Nick convinced his dad to buy the extra lumber they needed. On a flatbed trailer, pulled by his four-wheeled ATV, he made several trips to bring three ladders, about thirty old, but still usable, "two-by-fours," ten "two-by-sixes," a few "four-by-fours," and six sheets of half-inch plywood. The plywood was new, but the rest of the wood had laid next to their barn under a tarp for years.

The first thing they did was break into the cooler for munchies. Then Lori gave everyone a pencil and paper to sketch out their ideal fort.

Everyone liked Adam's artistic design the best. However, Nick's dad had to explain to them the importance of safety and strength over beauty. So after listening for a few minutes they decided to go with this practical approach.

Then the work began at a feverish pace.

First, Nick's dad measured and cut four four-by-fours to make a six-foot square floor support for the fort. While the boys held the boards in place he nailed them with spikes, up high, between the trunk of the tree and two heavy branches that faced south—the sunniest side. Meanwhile he guided the girls to measure and cut two-by-sixes to fit the four-by-four frame.

Again, while the boys held the boards in place, he hammered the nails to finish the solid floor.

The girls gathered the scrap pieces of wood, plus some extra twigs, and made roasting sticks as Amber's mom got a campfire going. After roasting and eating the hot dogs, they roasted the marshmallows over the embers.

When it got dark, the boys told ghost stories which spooked everyone.

After that, everyone went off to bed. The boys crawled into Nick's tent, and the girls, accompanied by Amber's mom, went off to sleep in theirs.

The next morning, for breakfast, they devoured the muffins and juice that Lori's mom had sent.

Then they measured, cut, and nailed together four five-foot-high walls that they then lifted with the pulley and rope onto the platform. They nailed through the two-by-sixes into the frame.

Once the walls were up and nailed together, Nick's dad instructed them to build five roof trusses to nail on top of the walls.

The children helped cut three windows and a door into four sawed pieces of plywood. One by one they pushed these up the ladders and nailed them to the wall studs to complete the walls. Once they put the plywood on the roof the "tight shell" was done!

Now, it was time for the children to add their finishing touches. They joyfully painted the inside and outside of the club house. After they waited for the paint to dry, they hung Adam's old tools. Then, they dragged up the old cushions from the sofa Cory's parents were throwing out, and the CD player donated by John's dad.

Kimmie brought along a disposable camera to capture, in pictures, their "tree-mendous" accomplishment, "Smile everyone and say 'tree!'"

The sun began to set, once again, by the time they finished. Exhausted, they were ready to go home for a bath, and to sleep in their *own* beds.

Chapter Five:
A Swim at the Quarry

It was very hot in the club house that following afternoon.

Nick had several beads of sweat running down his forehead. Everyone seemed ready for a swim, but Kimmie suggested it first. "Hey, why don't we all go jump into the quarry?"

"Yeah! Great idea," declared Amber. "Let's go!"

"Wait a minute," interrupted Mary. "We all need our bathing suits." She turned to the group's fastest runner and said, "Adam, why don't you run to all the boys' houses and get their swimming trunks and towels. I'll run to all the girls' houses and get their swim suits and towels. Okay?"

"Okay," Adam agreed. "Everyone else just head to the quarry. We'll meet up there." Then, turning to Mary, Adam challenged, "I bet I can beat you to the quarry."

"Never!" Mary replied. "I'll bet you a buck I'll be there before you."

Before Adam could say anything, Mary was already climbing down the tree-fort ladder. Adam followed quickly behind her, and everyone else "turtled" their way to their favorite swimming hole along the dusty path that led through the forest. This was the ideal way to escape this spring day's sweltering heat.

Adam ran to Nick's house first where he knew Nick's bathing suit had been drying on a clothesline strung across his backyard. The boy moved so fast that he almost forgot Nick's towel. Nick's mom saw him

from her kitchen window, and yelled, "What's going on Adam?"

"We're going swimming and Nick needs his bathing suit."

"What about a towel?" Nick's mom asked.

"Oh yeah. Right. I almost forgot," Adam said. "Where are your towels?"

"In the laundry room," she replied. "Let me get you one." She returned a minute later and handed over Nick's towel. The time lost seemed like eternity to Adam who immediately ran off yelling, "Thank you!"

Meanwhile, Mary met with similar consequences in her race to beat Adam. Most of the girls' bathing suits were hard to find. Some were neatly folded in dresser drawers, while others were stuffed in back packs or in laundry baskets.

The rest of the group had a much easier time. Kimberly had a few pictures left on her camera, so she took pictures of the others as they walked along the path, and as the children stopped to pick blueberries that grew on the bushes bordering the path.

The group finally got to the quarry, and all the children sat down on a large flat granite rock shaded by an old oak tree.

Thirty minutes later, Adam and Mary both arrived, amazingly at the same time, tying their race. Overheated and out of breath the two realized they had both lost compared to the others who had far more fun munching down wild blueberries along the way.

"Hey guys, did you save us some of those blueberries?" Adam asked.

Partly feeling ashamed they had forgotten their friends, Amber spoke for the group. "We're really sorry," she replied. "We forgot about you guys."

Adam complained with good cause, "We raced around to help all of you, and you forgot us?"

"Yeah, that's not very nice," Mary, the tom*girl*, added. "And by the way, not all of us are 'guys.'"

Lori and the others chuckled. "We'll make it up to you *guys*."

Chapter Six:
The Mysterious Old Cabin

After a cooling swim in the quarry, the group decided to return to the blueberry bushes to pick a bucket of berries for their neglected friends, Adam and Mary.

Along the way, John and Amber were attracted by a beautiful butterfly that beckoned them to venture off the forest trail and into the thickened woods. Suddenly, out of the corner of his eye, John spied a broken down cabin.

"Hey, will you get a load of that?" John said to Amber. Then they called for the others to join their investigation of the old building. "Hey you guys, come here! We found an old cabin."

"Where are you?" Kimberly called. "We can't see you."

"We're over here!" yelled Amber. "Over here!"

The children followed Kimmie in the direction of Amber's voice, and moments later they all stood in front of the abandoned cabin.

"I wonder who this place belongs to?" asked John. "I never knew this was here."

"It's spooky," said Mary.

Cory agreed, "Really! Almost all the doors and windows are all broken."

"Should we go inside and look around?" Adam bravely proposed.

"Yeah," Lori replied. "Maybe we'll find a treasure chest or something."

So, they decided to go inside the strange little house.

"Awesome!" Adam exclaimed when they got inside the main room. "I'll bet this is the living room."

"Yeah, and nobody's lived here for a hundred years," giggled Amber.

"Look over here," directed Nick. "Here's a little bedroom with a broken down wooden bed. There's even an old blanket and a pillow still on it.

"Cool!" said John as he and Lori entered the little room. "We can use this as another hide out."

Cory stepped over to the side of the bed and sat down. "Ouch!" he cried. "Something just stuck me."

Chapter Seven:
The Magical Map

Amber asked Cory, "What is it?"
"I don't know," Cory replied. "It felt like a piece of glass. It's stuck between this blanket and the wooden bed."

Nick pulled the old blanket back, and saw an old picture frame wedged into the inner side of the bed frame.

"Look here," said Cory. "It was broken glass! It's part of a picture frame with a map in it. It's stuck to the side of the bed."

"Try to get it out so we can see it," encouraged Kimberly.

"But, be careful," urged Amber. "Don't cut yourself."

Nick carefully removed the broken glass from the picture frame. The children quickly crowded around the old piece of parched paper.

"Looks like a treasure map," Mary declared.

"Yeah! It really does," seconded John.

The old map showed a path with a broken line directing its bearer from the old cabin through the woods to what appeared to be a wooden cross-hatched fence. Another path continued from there to another taller fence surrounding a meadow. The fence had a gate and then another path leading from the gate to a large tree

near the center of a field that merged with the meadow. Next to the tree was the word "Tlytiettlym." There were two hearts on this tree, one on its base and the other on its trunk. An arrow pointed from the word Tlytiettlym to the heart on the tree trunk. There were also a number of flowers drawn in the tree's branches, and more at the base of the tree surrounding the other heart.

"Let's follow the map and see if we can find this tree," Amber said.

"Really," said Kimberly. "Maybe the hearts show places where treasure is hidden!"

"Let's split any treasure we find evenly between us," urged Adam. "That way, no member of our club will feel bad or left out."

"Great!" said Mary.

So, the children left the strange cabin. They walked along the path for awhile, when suddenly they were met by the three members of the "mean team."

"Where are you guys going?" asked Courtney inquisitively.

"We've got a treasure map that we're following," replied Lori.

"A treasure map?" repeated Anthony, then he added, "You can't be serious."

"Yes, we are," Amber defended. "This is a real treasure map, and we're going to find this special tree. If you don't believe us, why don't you just come along and see for yourselves?"

"What? Amber, are you crazy? Inviting the 'dog pack' along on *our* treasure hunt doesn't sound like fun to me," Mary protested.

"Why should we go along with you anyway?" Courtney sneared. "Your map will probably lead us into a trap or somethin'."

Then Casey angrily challenged Courtney. "Why can't you ever be nice to them? I'm tired of the way you're always getting us into fights! And I'm quitting this club if you don't stop being so mean."

"That's fine with me," returned Courtney. "You go right ahead and quit."

"Anthony, you should think about quitting too," Casey urged. Then she added, "If you're always mean, then you'll never make it to heaven!"

"Well," replied Anthony, "I see your point." Then turning to Courtney, Anthony announced, "I'm quitting too. Bye, bye Courtney." With that the two protesters began to walk away.

"Fine!" Courtney called after them. "I'll have a club all to myself." Then she stomped off in a huff in the other direction leading back to town.

The eight members of the "cool kids club" simply stood there dazed. They were amazed. In front of their eyes their arch rivals—the "mean team"—ceased to exist.

As soon as Amber came to her senses, she called after Anthony and Casey, "Hey! Wait up you two! Why don't you join us? Come along with us to find the treasure!" Her seven friends followed, racing after the two club misfits.

Meanwhile, as Anthony, Casey and the rest of the group were making amends, Courtney wandered alone along the silent lonely forest road. *I'll show them*, she thought. *I'll get back at them for everything they said.*

Suddenly, as if all nature was against her, a grey-black cloud appeared in the sky over her head. The forest turned instantly dark. Then, strangely, huge rain drops began to fall from that bizarre cloud. They seemed to be focused on hitting and drenching Courtney's little head.

The rain pelted Courtney's dirty-blonde hair as if sent to extinguish her anger. *Maybe this was sent to wake me up from a nightmare*, she reasoned. Then, as the cloud and rain seemed to follow her a long way down the road, she realized, *It might not go away until I start being nice to the others.*

With that thought, the rain instantly stopped. The magical meaningful cloud simply vanished--went *poof.* It was gone.

How bizarre, she thought and then decided, *I better go catch up with the others.*

Now, the rest of the children had decided that they would give Courtney one more chance. They determined that she could join their club, so long as she behaved. So, when they looked back and saw her running toward them yelling, "Hey guys! Wait up! I'm coming too!" everyone felt better.

"I'm really sorry," Courtney said, noticeably out of breath from her run. "It wasn't very nice of me to say what I said about you tricking us. I'd like to join your treasure hunt, if you still want me."

Amber responded first, "Sure, Courtney. We already decided to invite you to join our club the next time we saw you."

"We'll behave ourselves," promised Anthony as he comically put his arm around Courtney's shoulders. "Really we will. No more fighting!"

After a few minutes of rest and peace-making, the group had gathered their energy to continue their journey.

"Okay," Adam affirmed after reexamining the map. "Let's get going. Everyone stay close together so no one gets lost."

Now united, the expanded troop eagerly searched to find the special tree drawn on the map. The one with flowers and hearts all around it—possibly depicting some very valuable treasures.

The first part of their journey took them along a trail that ran near the tree house. "By the way," Courtney conceded, "your tree house is the best I've ever seen."

Then the group followed the path as far as it went, precisely as the map showed. They walked for about half an hour until they came upon what appeared to be the first fence shown on the map. Most of the wooden fence posts were downed or rotted away. The wooden cross-hatches lay in a similar state of decay. The map showed a path leading from this fence to another one. The problem was that from here the path was so overgrown by tall grass and scrubby bushes that no one could find it.

"We'll just have to use our sense of direction from here," Mary said.

"The map should give us the general direction we need to take," reassured Amber.

So, the children used the map and their group's consensus to slowly make their way along the concealed path.

After awhile, the group came upon a wall of very high bushes that they could not see beyond.

"Now what?" asked Cory, with a bit of fatigue and frustration showing in his voice. "We've come all this way, and I'll bet we're lost."

"Yeah," said John, seeming disappointed. "We've been walking an awful long time."

"No way José," assured Lou. "We're not giving up now. For all we know, our treasure lies just beyond this wild hedge."

"That's it!" Adam realized. "This is a hedge. That's like the tall fence shown on the map."

"No, it can't be," John asserted. "The map clearly shows fence poles, not bushes or a hedge."

"Maybe someone planted this hedge after the map-maker died," Anthony reasoned. "Then the hedge grew up in front of the fence."

"Let's see if we can find our way to the other side," Mary suggested.

The children agreed on Anthony's rationale and Mary's plan to find a way through the tall thick hedge.

First they split up in two groups, each team scouting in opposite directions for an opening in the hedge. Unfortunately, there was no such thing to be found. The bush barrier was so thick, they couldn't even see through any part of it.

After regrouping about ten minutes later, Amber made a suggestion. "How 'bout if we choose a few spots and break some branches off the hedge to see if we can see anything?"

"Sure," Adam said. "Let's try it."

"Okay. Where do we start?" asked Casey.

"You're on your own," Adam challenged, going right to the task. "All right bush, take *that*," he said, as he pulled hard on a branch. The wood gave way to his strength.

Nick decided to try to break through the bush about ten yards beyond where Adam started.

The others followed Nick and spread out along the hedge about the same distances from each other.

A couple of minutes later Adam said, "I think I found something!"

"Really?" Courtney asked with curiosity peaked.

"What is it?" asked Mary.

Adam closely examined what he saw. "It's just a big old fungus stuck to the side of this large branch," he quipped disappointedly.

"I hate fungus!" Cory said.

The others resumed their efforts to penetrate the huge hedge.

A short while later, after more than a dozen branches were broken in her effort, Kimberly saw something gold shining near the middle of her part of the hedge. "Hey, you guys! Check this out."

All of the children came running over to see what Kimberly had discovered.

"What is it?" Lori questioned. "What did you find?"

"It looks like a door knob. In fact, I think it is a gold door knob. It looks like it's part of a fence gate. Let me pull away some of these other branches."

Seconds later, Kimmie further described what she saw. "It's a golden gate! It seems to run into a tall iron fence that runs through the back side of the hedge in both directions."

"Anthony, you were right!" Casey said. "The hedge must have grown up around the fence. But let's see this golden gate."

Everyone took their turn entering the cavern Kimberly had broken through the hedge. They each examined the gate and the special door knob that seemed to beckon them to pull.

"Let's clear the rest of these branches away and give this knob and gate a group tug," Amber said.

Everyone gathered around. "Now on the count of three," directed John, "—one, two, three." All the children tugged on the golden gate. As they did, it actually began to move—first slowly, and then easier and faster. Finally, the gate swung open, and as it did, a really bright light shown through the hedge. It was as if the light had been captured there for a thousand years and now, suddenly, was free to spill out over all the earth. The warm solar rays glowed on the faces of the eight club members and their new found friends who stood there in total disbelief. There, in that amazing moment, they suddenly beheld the beautiful meadow and adjacent field with one huge tree standing boldly near the middle.

Chapter Eight:
The Tlytiettlym Tree

The grand tree sparkled in the radiant sunlight. Its shimmering glow illuminated their faces as they made their way closer to their expected treasure. This was surely the most beautiful tree they had ever seen. It was perhaps the most glorious greenery in the whole wide world. As they drew nearer, they realized that much of its sparkling radiance came from the sun reflecting off the colorful fruit that adorned every branch.

Like the map showed, flowers were miraculously growing all over the tree. This floral array gave rise to the sweetest bounty of fruit, of every kind, from every part of the world. Likewise, around the base of the tree were flowers of all colors, shapes, and sizes. So plentiful were these flowers that as the children approached they became giddy from smelling their fragrances.

"This is like heaven," Lori giggled. "I've never seen such beautiful flowers."

"This tree can't be real," Casey said. "Someone pinch me to see if I'm dreaming."

"Look at all that fruit!" said Nick. "I bet there's every kind of species on the planet growing here. I don't understand how this one tree can grow all these different kinds of fruit."

"Do you think we can climb up and pick the fruit?" asked Mary.

"It all seems too high up," answered Cory. "How will we get up there?"

"We can boost each other up if we work together," urged Adam.

"What happens if one of us falls?" Kimberly questioned fearfully. "Someone might get hurt. Besides, how will we ever get help since we're so far away from home?"

"Don't be afraid," Anthony encouraged Kimmie. "We can do it if we're careful and work together."

"But what about the treasure?" Lori asked, recalling the primary reason they sought the tree. "I thought we came to discover some great hidden treasure shown by these hearts. Why don't we look for those hearts first before trying to figure out how to get to all this fruit?"

The children argued for a while about the challenges presented to them from their extraordinary discovery. Trying to decide what to do next, or even how to do it, turned out to be a major problem. The club members— previously "best friends"—now seemed unable to simply get along. Unable to reach a concensus about how to proceed in harvesting the fruit of this glorious tree, they argued and argued. It was as if the smell of the flowers had cast an evil spell on them that made them fight instead of cooperate or hate instead of love. But how could that be? Everything looked so beautiful!

"Maybe that's the point of all this fussing and fighting," Cory said. "Maybe the hearts on this map and all these beautiful surroundings are trying to tell us something about the real treasure here. Maybe these Tlytiettlym tree hearts relate to our hearts and our ability to share the fruits of our combined energy and efforts in working together to accomplish something here?"

"Well, think about it," Kimberly said, "We're all best friends. Now, suddenly we're fighting. We were able to build a whole club house, high up in a tree, by working together. We never argued once. Now, suddenly, we get here, surrounded by all this beauty, and we can't even decide what to do next because we're arguing so much."

"I get it," Courtney continued. "It's *so* beautiful here, that unless we measure up to *these* surroundings—the colors, flowers, smells, light and these loving hearts, depicted on this map—we won't be able to get anything accomplished."

"Absolutely cool," Lori asserted enthusiastically.

"Yeah! That really makes good *sense*," Mary acknowledged. "Maybe that's the true treasure of the Tlytiettlym tree—to teach us about *absolute love*."

"To get us to love each other rather than argue and fight," Adam added, grasping the positive assessment and building group spirit. "And then we can probably do anything and gain everything we want, here and now, and in the future too."

"There's magical powers expressed in love," Amber professed. "Maybe that's the Tlytiettlym tree's lesson for us."

"Yeah. Maybe that's all we need to harvest the fruit of all the earth," Casey said. "Love!"

"Love! Love! Love!" Anthony sang. "Haven't we heard that somewhere before?"

"Wait, I have an idea," proposed Mary. "Adam, you can lift Nick up on your shoulders." Then turning to Nick she continued, "Nick, you want to be an acrobat.

Now here's your chance. You stand on Adam's shoulders with your knees bent and your back braced against the tree trunk. The others will lift me up to you. Then you get me up to your shoulders where I can reach up and grab that first branch. Once there, I can pull Amber, Kimmie, Lori, Cory, and you up to my branch, and from there we can climb the rest of the tree to harvest the fruit."

"Great idea!" applauded Lori. "Let's do it!"

Quickly, without hesitation, and without any close calls, the children actualized Mary's plan.

Once in the tree, Nick, Kimberly, Amber, Lori and Cory carefully climbed the Tlytiettlym tree's branches. They harvested, one-by-one, the delicate fruit. Each piece was dropped softly and precisely into the secure hands of Casey, John, Courtney, Adam, Anthony and Mary.

"Casey, here's a mango," called Kimberly. "Catch."

"Anthony, come get this starfruit," yelled Amber.

Cory announced, "Here's a pomegranate. Come catch it Courtney!"

Working together in this way, the tree was soon harvested without any of the fruit being ruined, or any children being harmed. Once done, the fruit pickers simply climbed back down the way they got up.

The next day, the children returned with their parents, a couple of ATVs towing trailers, and a dozen wooden crates to cart the fruit back to their village.

On the way, Amber asked everyone, "What should we do with all of this gorgeous fruit?"

"I've already been thinking about it," said Lori. "Let's give ten pieces to every family in our community. I'm sure they'll like it a whole bunch."

"Great plan!" exclaimed Nick, and the others agreed.

"We'll help feed the poor people," concluded Cory. "I'm sure there's enough to share with everyone."

So, that's what they did. The children went from house to house distributing all the delicious Tlytiettlym tree fruit, and all the people in their beautiful New England town were grateful.

Within a few days, the townspeople realized something completely astonishing was occurring in all the people in their community. It seemed as though everyone got along better. Even better, all of the people who were sick at the time they ate the fruit, miraculously healed. Crippled people in wheelchairs stood up and walked again. Dying people with cancer stopped dying and began to smile. Every child with autism, who ate of the fruit, became well again.

And that's the end of this story.

Author Acknowledgments

I want to thank the following people for helping me with *The Tlytiettlym Tree*—my first published book: My mom, Jackie, who helped me learn to use the *Thesaurus* and helped me edit this story. My teacher, Ms. Julie McCallan, who taught me basic drawing and painting skills and tells many wonderful stories in class. My sister, Aria, and my classmates at the Waldorf school, who encouraged me to finish the illustrations in this book. Mary De La Fuenta who helped me greatly with these drawings and taught me additional drawing and coloring techniques. Last, but not least, I want to thank my dad, Leonard, for taking me with him to Philadelphia, where I got the idea for this story, and Washington, where I learned about autism and how we can help autistic children and their families.

About the Author

Alena Netia Horowitz was born June 1, 1992 in Beverly, Massachusetts. From a very young age she was extremely interested in art. Here she is, age 3, surrounded by her drawings.

Alena attends the Waldorf School in Sandpoint, Idaho where art and language skills are stressed. At the time of this writing, she was in the fourth grade.

Alena studies dance and takes guitar, flute, and violin lessons.

The town's swim coach said she "swims like a fish." Her favorite water sport is snorkeling with sea turtles and other ocean life. She is also an avid snow skier who

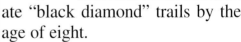

proudly learned to negoti-

ate "black diamond" trails by the age of eight.

Alena, age nine in this picture, lives with her parents, Jackie and Leonard Horowitz, her younger sister Aria, and her baby brother Aaron, in a river valley home, with an organic orchard and garden, in the mountains of northern Idaho.

The Tlytiettlym Tree

The Tlytiettlym Tree